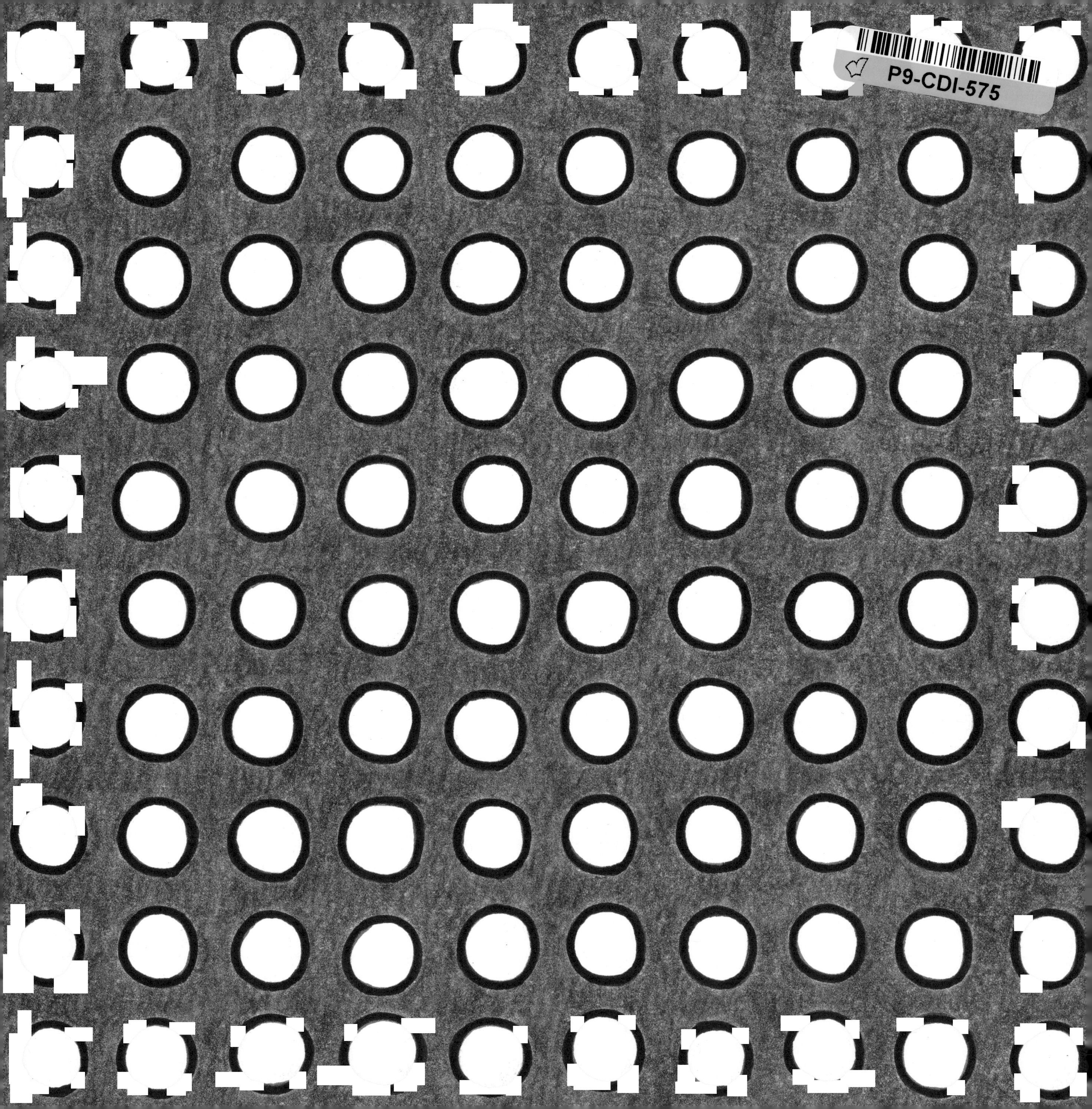

Kitten's First Full Moon

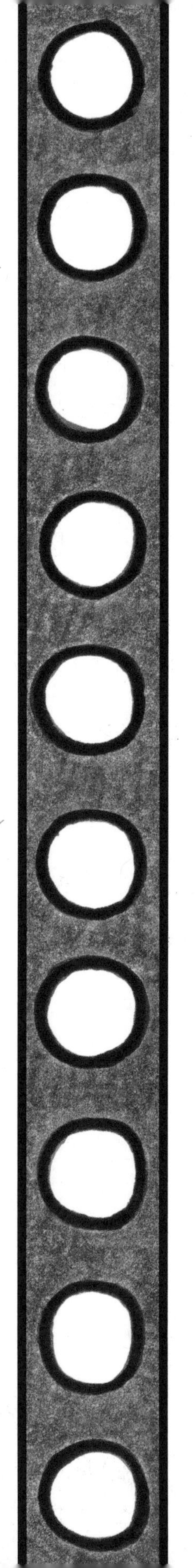

KEVIN HENKES

Kitten's First Full Moon

For L, W, C & S

For information, address HarperCollins Children's Books, a division of HarperCollins Publishers, 10 East 53rd Street, New York, NY 10022.
www.harperchildrens.com. Gouache and colored pencil were used to prepare the full-color art. The text type is 22-point Gill Sans Extra Bold.

Library of Congress Cataloging-in-Publication Data. Henkes, Kevin. Kitten's first full moon / by Kevin Henkes.—p. cm.—"Greenwillow Books."
Summary: When Kitten mistakes the full moon for a bowl of milk, she ends up tired, wet, and hungry trying to reach it.
ISBN 978-0-06-058828-1 (trade). ISBN 978-0-06-058829-8 (lib. bdg.) [1. Cats—Fiction. 2. Animals—Infancy—Fiction. 3. Moon—Fiction.] I. Title.
PZ7.H389Ki 2004 [E]—dc21 2003012564

11 12 13 WOR First Edition 20

It was Kitten's first full moon.
When she saw it, she thought,
There's a little bowl of milk in the sky.
And she wanted it.

So she closed her eyes

and stretched her neck

and opened her mouth and licked.

But Kitten only ended up

with a bug on her tongue.

Poor Kitten!

Still, there was the little bowl

of milk, just waiting.

So she pulled herself together

and wiggled her bottom

and sprang from the top step of the porch.

But Kitten only tumbled—

bumping her nose and banging her ear

and pinching her tail.

Poor Kitten!

Still, there was the little bowl

of milk, just waiting.

So she chased it—
down the sidewalk,
through the garden,
past the field,
and by the pond.
But Kitten never seemed to get closer.
Poor Kitten!

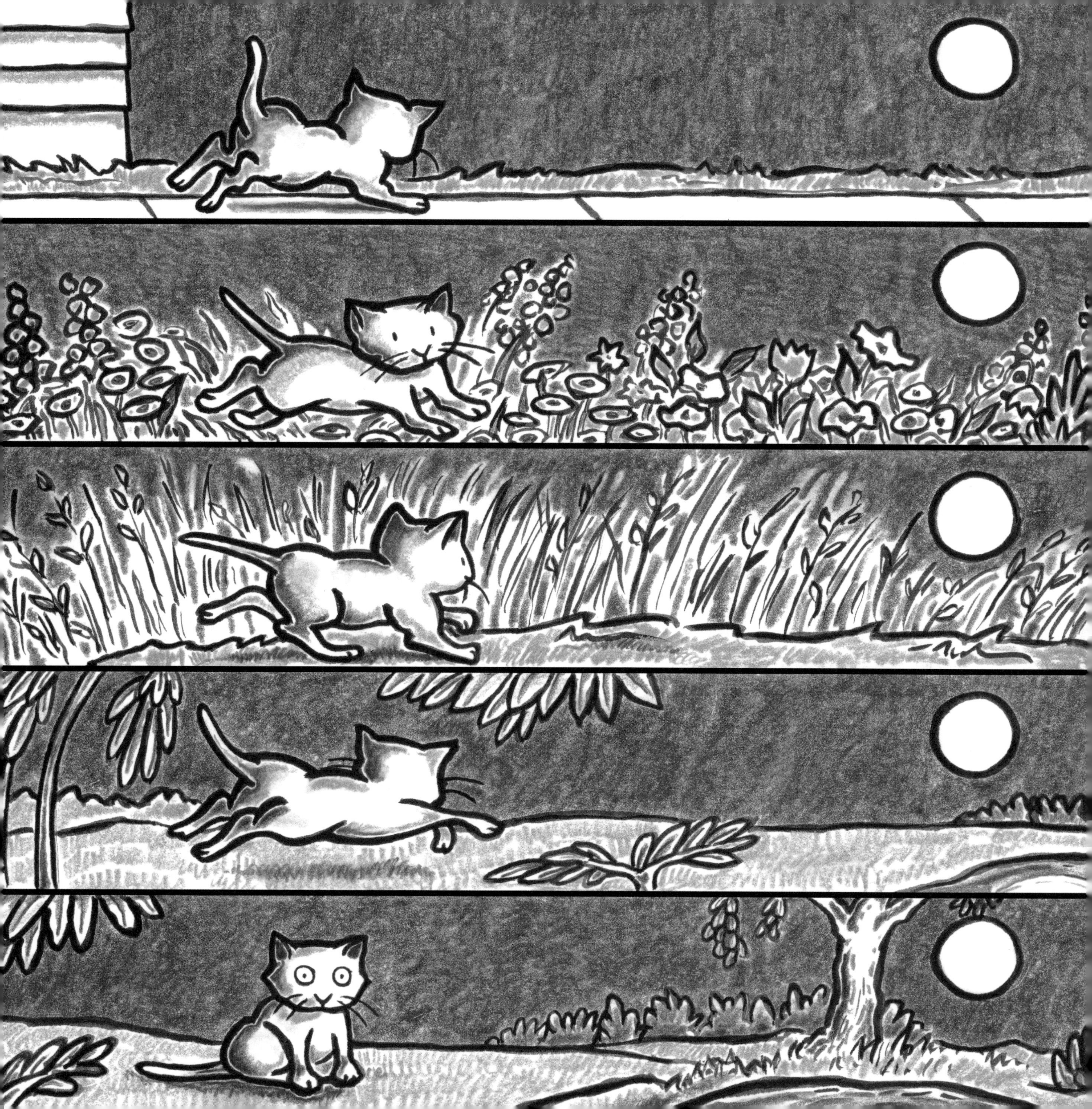

Still, there was the little bowl

of milk, just waiting.

So she ran

to the tallest tree

she could find,

and she climbed

and climbed

and climbed

to the very top.

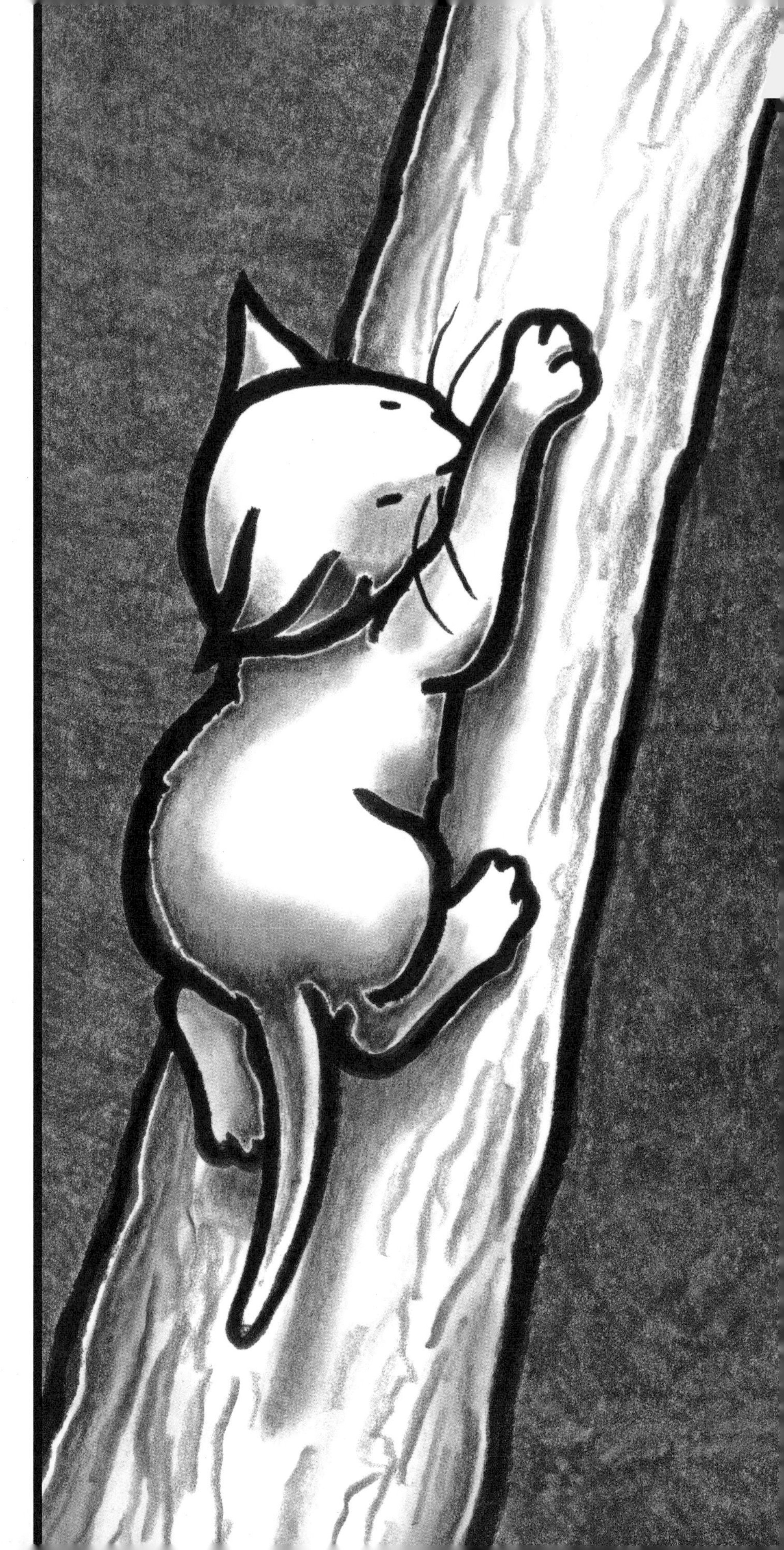

But Kitten
still couldn't reach
the bowl of milk,
and now she was
scared.
Poor Kitten!
What could she do?

Then, in the pond, Kitten saw
another bowl of milk.
And it was bigger.
What a night!

So she raced down the tree

and raced through the grass

and raced to the edge of the pond.

She leaped with all her might—

Poor Kitten!

She was wet and sad and tired and hungry.

So she went back home—

and there was

a great big

bowl of milk

on the porch,

just waiting for her.

Lucky Kitten!

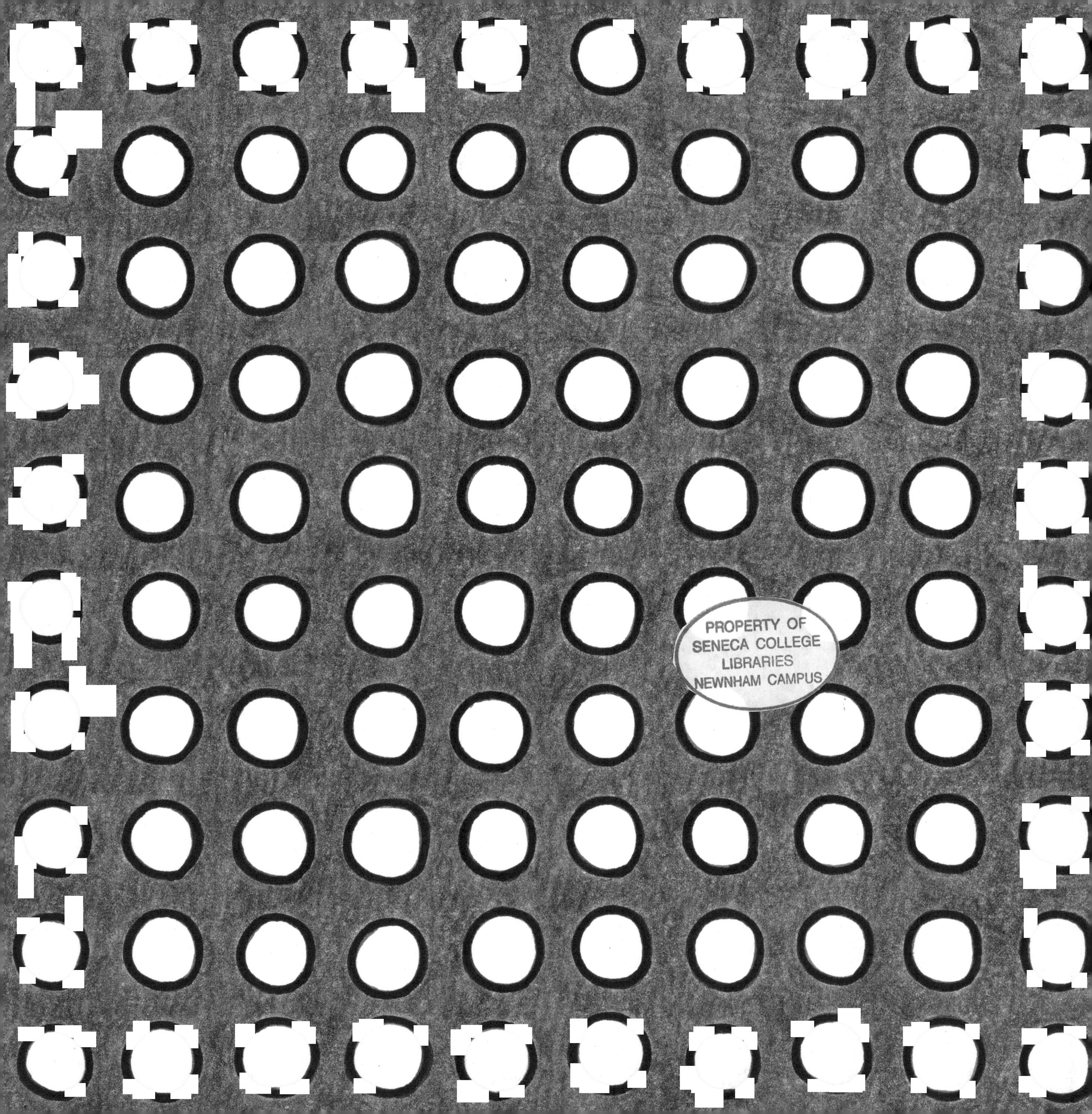